THE BLUE BUS

Walter W Mason

Copyright © 2025

Walter W Mason

eBook ISBN: 979-8-89795-352-3
Paperback ISBN: 979-8-89795-353-0
Hardcover ISBN: 979-8-89795-354-7

Leigh wanted to buy me a special birthday gift.

She'd been told a shop in the city had exactly what she wanted.

"Just walk down and cross at the crossing."

I said, "then back up to the bus stop."

"Catch the blue bus. It will take you to the city centre."

Leigh seemed doubtful.

"Please come with me."

Our first date was spent sitting with her mother in their car outside our school dance. Leigh had been a naughty girl and was grounded at the time.

It should have been an awkward night, but it was not. Even at 15 years and 8 months old, I knew I wanted Leigh to be my girl.

The following weekend, the church youth group had an outing at Crystal Creek. I was invited. Naturally, I was keen to go. A full day with Leigh. Even the possibility of time alone in secluded spots around the creek.

The day arrived. We stood on the old bridge. Our first kiss was short. Her little sister appeared. Sent by Leigh's mother to chaperone us. As I quickly pulled my arm from around her shoulder, I caught her earring on my sleeve and dislodged it. I unhooked the earring and dropped it into my pocket. I now had an excuse to go to Leigh's house the next day to return the earrings.

I persuaded an older friend to drive me the seven kilometres down to her house in Cordelia – Thank you, Gale and thank you for being a romantic. Your suggestion that Leigh and I would get married was exactly what happened.

I had no way of getting home but was prepared to walk and hitchhike, just to spend time with Leigh.

Luckily, Leigh's mother volunteered to drive me home. We sat in the back seat, and as we approached my house, she kissed me, and I knew I was in love with a girl who loved me.

———————————————

Leigh came to drive me home from work. She should have been at work herself. I asked if anything was wrong. She didn't answer. I asked if it had been a good day. She said,

"Not for me. They say I cannot do my job anymore."

She was a prison officer – a demanding, stressful job that she seemed to enjoy.

"Why?" I asked.

She was told she was not coping. In any given situation, she was losing her temper, and her decision-making ability.

I became concerned.

I started to research dementia. Signs of the disease had surfaced in Leigh's mother's family. I didn't really believe that dementia symptoms were appearing. She had always been emotional and quick-tempered. I was in a world of denial. Our life went on for another 12 months until I started discussing a work colleague. On more than one occasion, we went out to dinner with him and his wife. Even though we had spoken with him five days before, Leigh had a blank expression. She had no memory of him.

Because Leigh lived so far from me and all I had was a broken bicycle, we had to rely on school to see each other.

For both of us, the school year was grade ten. It was the year of the junior public exam. We needed to study. She studied a lot more than I did. I found myself drawing hearts with our names on them. I carved LEIGH into school desks and was threatened with severe caning from the school principal for damaging school property.

I did manage to persuade my friend Gale to take me down to Cordelia a second time. Leigh and I helped her mother paint and lay new laminate on the kitchen table.

Once again, I was driven home by her mum, and we grabbed the opportunity to hug and kiss in the back seat.

The exams were only a couple of hours each day. The English exam finished at 11 AM. Leigh had to wait until 3.30 to catch the bus home. I asked if she would like to have lunch with me.

She smiled, "Where do you want to go in our school uniforms?"

I suggested we go to Johnny's Fish Bar for hamburgers.

That was our first real date alone together and paid for by me.

The week before my father had given me some money. That was an unusual occurrence. He said it was for being a diligent student and for sitting the junior exam. The next day, I went to a local jeweler and bought a ring for Leigh. Not very expensive but she still has it.

I gave it to her in the Fish Bar. She cried.

By now, I was really becoming concerned. Normal discussion was almost impossible. The Prison Service was demanding a diagnosis so they could finalize her employment.

Our GP referred Leigh to a neurologist/dementia specialist, who took rehems of notes and referred her to a university clinic.

The clinic put Leigh through hours of memory and cognitive tests. I sat with her for the first test until the doctor gently explained that my wife was being examined, not both of us.

Leigh came out of more than one test crying. It was a very upsetting and sad day.

The university clinic specialist took us into her office to give us the results of the tests. For Leigh, time was short.

Anything she had set her mind on doing in her life, she should do it now.

We talked as we took the train home from the university. I asked Leigh what had upset her so much. She said they read lists and asked her to repeat them. She started to cry and said the whole thing was stupid. I was terribly upset. People who made my wife cry suffered my anger, but not in this case. Although I didn't let her see, I had tears in my own eyes.

No more smoking and no alcohol should be the rule. Souvenaid was recommended. I bought two cartons and also a large quantity of coconut oil, which the rumour had as being mentally beneficial. I knew I was grasping at straws, but I had to try.

I was no longer in denial. In fact, from that time on, I watched her behaviour closely. The specialist warned against Leigh driving and as it was her vehicle, she wanted to continue to drive. The car was leased, so I had to invent an end-of-lease scenario to have it taken away.

The exams were the end of the school year for us.

As was the practice then, we both found temporary work until Christmas. Leigh worked at Coles, and I worked in a soft drink factory. It was difficult, but we occasionally had lunch together. They were good times. We enjoyed the experience of an adult, wage-earning life. When my job finished a few days before Christmas, I haunted Coles to the extent of being told not to stop the staff from working.

At that time, I used my wages to buy a Christmas present from the local jeweller. It was a gold bracelet with two hearts, and I had our names engraved on them.

Christmas with our respective families was the normal celebration. For us, it lacked what was now special in our lives. Each other.

The supposed science told of keeping the mind active. Crossword puzzles and reading were the things that would help. Leigh had read all her life, A lot of the time instead of watching TV. She had been a devotee of difficult crosswords and logic puzzles for 20 years. The science has no basis.

Now, Leigh would stare at the puzzles and make no attempt to complete them. I bought the easier puzzles. Word circle, etc., and for a time, she was coping with these. Then I noticed she was not touching the new puzzles. I took out the magazine and started doing a puzzle, then asked her to help. She showed no interest. I now understood I was seeing the future. I didn't have any idea what I could do. I couldn't find any advice. Our GP referred Leigh to a geriatric specialist, who was sympathetic but had no answers to my questions. She advised me to ensure Leigh was eating well and, if that wasn't the case, to give her a protein supplement. I arrived home from that consultation and wondered what I could do. I could think of nothing. I worried for our future.

I had always removed the child-proofing features from containers. A few nights after the specialist consultation, Leigh vomited while I was showering. She had just brushed her teeth. Naturally, I was concerned and asked what was wrong. She didn't answer and vomited again. I took her into bed and brushed my own teeth. The mouthwash bottle was half full in the morning. Now, it was empty. I knew then she'd drunk almost half a bottle. I was horrified!

From that time on, I locked away or hid whatever poisons that were in the house.

We both went into year 11 at school the next year. It started as a good year. Leigh's junior marks were very good. Mine was not so good, but I was made house captain and was planning my year around that and meeting Leigh every day.

I received a letter telling me I had been accepted into the Justice Department's Magistrates Court office. I didn't really want to take the job. I would have preferred to stay at school. Dad wanted me to accept the position. He said no matter how far my schooling went, including university, I wouldn't find a better job. Public servants were reasonably well paid, and the conditions were without equal, including Government superannuation. I admit I didn't understand what superannuation involved. I knew it could never compensate for not seeing Leigh every day at school.

I had just turned 16 and lived at home. I had always followed my father's advice. Now, I didn't want to, but I still accepted the job offer.

Leigh was upset. She'd also been planning a year of being with me every day, and she admitted she was going to persuade me to study harder. Eventually, she accepted my decision to leave school and pleaded with me to find a way to come to see her every weekend.

After settling in, I found I was enjoying my new job. My work colleagues were helpful, and we became friends. I even managed to persuade one to drop me at Leigh's house every Friday on his way home from work. Leigh's mother or father would drive me home every Sunday night.

The situation must have been inconvenient for them, but they didn't complain.

I started to encourage Leigh to watch TV with me.

Covid and lockdowns arrived and upset lives the world over.

We tried to get some sunshine by sitting on our front porch. I was outside when I heard Leigh calling my name. When I came, she was sitting on the floor at the bottom of the stairs. Her left foot was up near her knee. I don't know how I felt. I suppose I panicked. I ran up to a neighbour's house and explained that Leigh slipped on the stairs. We straightened her leg. She didn't express much pain. She was always very strong.

The surgeon told me Leigh would need major surgery. The hospital was in lockdown, so I couldn't see her. I needed a shoulder to cry on. I didn't have one. I had lost my shoulder forever!

When, eventually, I was allowed to go to the hospital to bring her home, she was different. More vague, more unsure. I believe the anaesthetic caused an escalation of her dementia.

Leigh continued at school. She told me she didn't want to be there. She no longer cared about education.

Sometimes, when her mother came to town to do the grocery shopping, she would pick Leigh up after school to help with the groceries, and if Leigh was able, she would call into the office where I worked to say hello. She charmed the work colleague who drove me down to see her on Fridays. I smiled. I knew what she was doing. He probably did, too, but he was a nice man and continued to drive me.

The year went on in this fashion. Hormones were raging. I seemed to have grown extra hands. Luckily, I was kept at arm's length.

Toward the end of the year, my Father was going to Cairns to prepare the house he built in Edge Hill for sale. Mom thought it would be nice for us to spend the weekend in Cairns. We stayed in a motel. We had separate but adjoining rooms. That night, Leigh came into my room. We spent the night together.

We had a motel breakfast together in my room, extremely tough steak and eggs. We were laughing at Leigh's attempt to cut the steak when Mom came into the room. She gave me an accusing stare. I avoided looking at her. I think she could see the guilt on my face. It didn't matter. That night was the most wonderful experience of my life.

We lived downstairs for a month. Then I found Leigh climbing the stairs to get to the bathroom. She'd become single-minded about getting upstairs. I installed rails in the stairwell, and we moved back upstairs.

At this time, I was choosing Leigh's clothes and helping her to dress. Her leg was healing well. As had always been the case, she healed rapidly and soon discarded her walker. I was concerned that she might fall. I felt incredibly upset and guilty because I knew the stairs were slippery. I'd already ordered anti-slip tape, but it didn't arrive until a week after her accident.

Leigh worked hard to exercise her leg. She wasn't going to allow a badly broken leg to interfere with her life. I walked beside her in case she stumbled. She looked at me as if I was a nuisance. She had never needed help, and it was no different now.

I was still choosing her clothes and helping her dress. I was surprised she accepted this without fuss. When she had the chance to select her own clothing, she picked anything. It was a cold winter, but she would take out shorts and a flimsy top. Anything that came to hand. When I picked something warmer, she didn't object. This wasn't normal behaviour. She'd always tried to be independent.

Shortly after, she regained almost full use of her leg, and we began to do the grocery shopping together. The walk was around ten minutes so it wasn't difficult for her, and if it was, she didn't complain. In the supermarket, I'd notice strange things in the trolley. I had to take them out and slip them onto a nearby shelf without her noticing. The supermarket staff must have been puzzled when they found coffee with vitamins, etc.

Then came the day Leigh vanished.

After we dropped Leigh at home back in Ingham, Mom gave me an accusing look as only she could.

"Leigh's mother said she wasn't concerned when Leigh is with us. Does she have reason to be concerned?"

I shrugged; I didn't know what to say.

When I rang Leigh, as I did most evenings, I told her what Mom said. She wasn't worried. She told me the weekend in Cairns was the only thing she wanted to think about. I tried to be practical with the motive of encouraging more occasions like the weekend we just had. I said we'd have to talk about contraception. Leigh told me not to worry. She would somehow get a prescription for the pill.

That didn't happen, nor could we find the time to be alone. It certainly wasn't for the lack of trying. I spent every weekend at Leigh's house. Her mother set up a canvass stretcher in the living room. It may have been a calculated move. Every time I moved, the damn thing would make a terrible noise. Between that and her sisters constantly spying, we were becoming frustrated.

The next Saturday, we were invited to my cousin's wedding. We managed to sneak out early and go to my house. We were both excited, and we took advantage of being alone.

I'd been warned that Leigh may wander. I kept the house locked, and the keys where they always were in my work bag. Feeling the effects of stress and 40 years of smoking, I was very tired. Leigh was now intermittently incontinent. I left her downstairs watching TV while I cleaned the bedroom and changed the sheets. When I came down, I couldn't find her. The security door was open, and she wasn't in the house. I ran out into the street, but I couldn't see her in any direction. I hurried along the street and into the side street toward the supermarket. I couldn't see her. When I reached the supermarket, I frantically searched and questioned the staff – many of whom knew her. She hadn't been seen. I hurried back past our house in the other direction to the nearest side street. I couldn't see her. I rang my family in panic. They came out and started to search for her. After an hour, I went to the police and told them the story. They promised to send a car to search. It had been two hours. I was still walking the streets when the police rang and told me to go home in case she turned up there.

A sergeant came to my house and sat with me. The situation was horrible. I wanted to keep looking. He told me to sit down and wait.

After more than three hours, he received a phone call. Someone had seen her in their front yard. She was cleaning their car. They approached her but couldn't understand what she was saying so they rang the police and a car was sent. She left that house and walked across the street into a park, where she sat on a bench. It was seven kilometres from home, and I think she must have been very tired.

The sergeant drove me to the park. When Leigh saw me, she waved and hurried over to me. I hugged her and had tears in my eyes. It was a devastating day.

Our world was almost perfect. Two kids in love without any worries. I know we should have been more careful, but we weren't. The possibility of a baby wasn't something that concerned us at all. Our second Christmas was coming. Leigh's parents planned to take a holiday driving to Victoria to see relatives. They would be away for almost four weeks. We had to accept that this would be a considerable time apart. When you're sixteen, four weeks is forever.

I wrote letters to the address Leigh gave me, but I couldn't ring her. She sent letters to me with some photographs, and these made me miss her more than ever.

During this time, I turned 17 and got my driver's license. I promised myself that we would never be separated again, and we never were.

Leigh rang me from Townsville. They were spending two days at a family friend's house before coming home. She asked if I could come down to Townsville. I told her somehow I would. I hadn't driven such a distance on my own before, and when I asked Dad if I could take his new Toyota Land Cruiser station wagon to Townsville, he was very doubtful. He'd had it just a few months, and it was only the second such vehicle sold in North Queensland. Surprisingly he finally said yes.

In 15 minutes, I was on my way to see Leigh for the first time in four weeks. I was keen, but I drove very carefully.

A 17-year-old on his way to see his love!

—————————

Since that day, I have always kept the house keys in my pocket.

Leigh was rapidly losing the ability to communicate. My heart was breaking as I watched her looking at me and trying to form the words she wanted. She would catch sight of her mother's photograph on the shelf, smile and say, Mom.

Then came the devastating Saturday morning when she had her first seizure.

We were watching TV. Leigh suddenly snapped forward with her arms outstretched and stiff. She was making strange growling noises. I was totally shocked. I rang the ambulance in panic. I must have sounded incoherent. They told me to sit down, take a breath, and speak slowly. I didn't know. I thought she was having a stroke. I couldn't find anything to do but hold her and say something. I don't know what I was saying. I did know I was frightened and felt totally helpless.

The ambulance arrived. They were very calm. They gave her some tests and told me she didn't have a stroke. She had probably experienced a seizure, and I shouldn't be alarmed. I insisted they take Leigh to the hospital. This was probably a mistake. The doctors subjected her to hours of tests and scans. She was upset and frightened. Eventually, I was told she didn't have a true seizure. I still don't know what type of seizure she had and what a true seizure was. I did know she had a seizure and went on to have three more over the next few weeks.

We went to our GP. He prescribed anti-seizure medication for Leigh and anti-depression medication for me. He asked if I was coping. I said I was. What else could I do? At this stage, he mentioned that I should be prepared for Leigh to go into a nursing home. I didn't want this to happen and promised myself it never would. Who else could care for her as well as I could?

When I arrived at the house where they were staying, Leigh ran out to meet me. I opened the door almost knocking her over. The scene must have appeared comical. The Toyota was a high-clearance vehicle, and Leigh was jumping up, trying to hug me before I could get out. Her father and his mate, watching from the front veranda, were laughing. We didn't care. I climbed out, and we hugged and kissed. I desperately wanted to do a lot more. Somehow, that would have to wait.

Later, Leigh's mother wanted to get some laundry done. She was never pleased to have clothing waiting to be washed. This trait was passed to Leigh, who actually enjoyed doing laundry and would sniff the items when they dried with a satisfied look on her face.

Leigh told her Mum we'd do the laundry and hang the cloths. We finally had time to be alone together in the downstairs laundry room.

The 90-minute drive home became a two-hour-plus drive. We told each other everything that happened over the past four weeks. A few minutes before reaching her home, I turned into a secluded area where we were able to hug and kiss in private for ten minutes or so.

Before school started, Leigh decided she would find a job and not go back. Her aunt was Lucinda Post Mistress, and Leigh had been working at odd times in the telephone exchange. Her Aunt now offered Leigh a full-time telephonist job. We talked over the offer, which meant Leigh would live with her grandparents at Lucinda during the week. My father offered to buy me an old car a few days before, so we decided the Telephonist job should be accepted.

Other people were now advising me to consider a nursing home, including the Geriatric specialist. I accepted this advice without comment, but I knew there was no possibility of this happening. A month passed without any seizures, but the medication seemed to be making Leigh stubborn and violent. She refused to go to bed at night, and when I insisted by gently pushing her into the bedroom. She bit me very forcefully. The bite made me angry. It was the first time I'd allowed my anger to surface, and I had to deliberately close my eyes and tell myself it wasn't something she wanted to do and that the medication had changed her.

I rang the doctor and he emailed me a new prescription. Her attitude changed and she eventually calmed and became her normal, loving self.

I knew I was smoking excessively. A sudden noise startled me like never before. Even the unexpected closing of a nearby car door made me flinch.

I wondered if my approach could be better for her. I could find no useful advice, and when I became exasperated, I simply sat down and smoked.

There were a lot of suggestions regarding things I felt weren't very useful. Home health care were sending a regular cleaner. Buying meals at a much-reduced rate was put forward. The advice was well-intentioned, but cooking meals was an easy thing that Leigh had done for me for a long, long time.

Leigh was now totally incontinent and I was helping her to shower. None of this was a burden. It meant we couldn't go walking nor could I go to the supermarket. She was physically more unstable and had bruising on her arms because she bumped furniture and walls. I always walked beside her. I was determined to be there whenever she stumbled. I realised my beautiful wife's quality of life depended entirely on me.

We settled into a routine. I drove down to Lucinda on Wednesday evenings, and we would walk along the beach. I bought a very large beach towel, and we went to our favourite secluded place to lie down and pass a wonderful hour alone together with no cares or demands to bother us. I would Take Leigh back home on Friday nights and spend the weekend at her house. Even when Leigh was required to work occasional weekends, I'd go fishing while she worked and drive her home at night. I couldn't imagine our lives being any better. That was about to change.

She rang me at work one Tuesday and told me to come to Lucinda that night. She had some news for me. I naturally wanted to know what the news was. She wouldn't tell me, and just before she hung up the phone, she started to cry.

As soon as I finished work, I drove to Lucinda to see her.

Her grandmother made a sponge cake. This wasn't unusual. There was always a fresh cake or scones when I came to Leigh's grandparents' house.

We went down to the beach. I kept asking what the news was. I couldn't see anything wrong with Leigh and was mystified.

Eventually, on the beach, she hugged me and asked me not to be angry. I kissed her and told her I wasn't angry. She wouldn't let go, and I asked if she was sick. She said she wasn't sick; she was pregnant. I think I said something like Shit. She pushed me away and started crying. I don't really remember how I felt apart from being shocked. Still crying she asked me what we were going to do. I had no answer. We walked hand in hand back up the beach. I realised we were both only seventeen. I couldn't legally marry until I was eighteen.

Leigh was saying she needed to tell her parents. I dreaded the moment but both our parents would need to know.

The confession wasn't as traumatic as we believed it would be. Apparently, Leigh's parents, because of rumours, had expected the news. Mine hadn't, but were understanding. We told them we wanted to marry. The next day, my father talked to the magistrate, who was actually my boss. He called me into his office and explained, very firmly, that I was a stupid young lad who should have known better. Because he knew me and knew I was reliable, he was prepared to hear an application for an underage marriage. Then he grinned and told me not to worry.

Leigh always had coffee and two pieces of toast with vegemite, along with some fruit for breakfast. I was letting her sleep for as long as she liked. Up until this time she got herself out of bed. I could hear her moving upstairs and would go up to bring her down. Now, she couldn't get out of bed unassisted, so I'd go up every fifteen minutes to check if she was awake. If so, I'd help her out of bed, into the shower, and then walk with her slowly down the stairs.

She was now ignoring the toast. I put strawberries, grapes, and slices of banana or orange on a plate for her. We watched TV, and she very slowly ate some fruit. It wasn't enough. I didn't realise she could no longer swallow properly. She'd been refusing to eat lunch for more than a week, and in the evenings, she would eat only mashed potatoes. I tried meat cut into small pieces. Leigh would chew one piece of meat endlessly and wouldn't touch corn kernels'. Chips and gravy were always her favourite. She put a chip into her mouth one night and chewed for so long I told her to spit it out. She wouldn't do that. I didn't want her to go to bed with the chip still in her mouth. I waited almost an hour. When I tried to check in her mouth, she bit my finger. We had to go to bed. I lay beside her, watching. I couldn't think of anything more I could do. I thought eating would not ever be a problem. I understood yogurt and mashed potato wouldn't be enough. A nurse later told me that I should have given her baby food.

For the first time I began to think I was failing.

From the moment I received court permission to marry, everything was hectic. We went to see the Methodist Minister, Whom we both knew well from our connection with the Methodist Youth Fellowship. He was very relaxed about the situation, and he took us downstairs to show us the boat he was building. He knew Leigh and I had been together for two years. He asked if we believed we had a permanent relationship and if we understood the implications of marriage. We must have assured him of our commitment. He said our marriage was completely acceptable to him and the church.

With the church booked, I thought my responsibilities were over. Leigh had other ideas. I had to buy wedding and engagement rings, book a motel for our one-night honeymoon, and find somewhere for the wedding reception. I had 70 dollars in the bank. That went on the wedding ring. Thankfully, Dad had an engagement ring made with one of his own gemstones set in it.

Leigh had almost two hundred dollars in her bank. She paid for the honeymoon room. I hadn't realised the Minister needed paying. Leigh took care of that. She suggested the reception be held in a function hall at Lucinda, and we were given a very good rate for the venue. There were, to my mind, endless discussions about wedding and bridesmaid dresses. Apparently, my input wasn't needed, luckily, because I had no idea. Already the future pattern of our life together was set. Leigh would take care of me for more than 50 years. We had to go to her grandparents and tell them they were going to be great-grandparents. Her grandmother made scones, and her grandfather nodded his acceptance and had a cup of tea. Leigh had an understanding family.

I'd been giving Leigh water and various fruit juices along with coffee. Now, she wasn't drinking. I had to hold the cup to her lips and basically bully her into drinking. She didn't seem to be drinking enough.

I checked wherever I could. I couldn't find any advice except the sufferer may find it easier to drink from a straw. Leigh didn't know what the straw was. I showed her repeatedly, and she seemed to use it sporadically. I was still worried she wasn't getting enough fluid. I'll admit I didn't know what to do. I'd always believed I was very masculine. Not showing emotion was how I was brought up. Emotions were to be controlled in a masculine fashion. I cried; I couldn't stop myself. Leigh's total dependence on me was heartbreaking. I had no idea how I could continue. At no time did I think it would be like this. I don't know what I believed it would be, but now I understand that what I was doing wasn't enough.

I spoke to the Home Healthcare nurse and asked if she could come to see Leigh. She agreed to come the following day.

The next morning, I helped Leigh out of bed, but she was unable to stand. I put her back to bed and rang to ask if the nurse could come straightaway.

The nurse examined Leigh and questioned me regarding the last couple of weeks. She told me Leigh was dehydrated and undernourished. I would have to call the ambulance. The ambulance officers arrived and administered some tests. They said Leigh would need to be taken to hospital. She would certainly need to be kept in for a time. I asked if Leigh would be able to return home. They were noncommittal. I knew no matter how hard I tried, I hadn't given her the care she required. I now believed that our life together was over. In front of all those people, I cried.

Our wedding took place, and according to everybody, was a success. We left after 11 PM. At that time, there was a low-level crossing over a tidal creek that flooded during extremely high tides. On our wedding night, there was an extremely high tide. I drove straight into the water. This wasn't in our plans. Nevertheless, we both exclaimed

"Oh shit!" And laughed.

I pushed the car through the tidal water, wondering if the ripples and swirls were crocodiles. Leigh steered and shouted encouragement. When we finally reached our honeymoon motel, we collapsed on the bed with a bottle of champagne, even though neither of us was old enough to drink legally. I leant over to Kiss Leigh and was spiked by a piece of wire. Her hair was held in place by dozens of them.

We were both extremely tired. We drank the champagne and slept the night among bits of wire.

We were happy. We were together.

I'll be with you on the blue bus

We'll sit together always